Magic
Toyshop

For Ruby

Special thanks to Val Wilding

First published in 2012
by Faber and Faber Ltd
Bloomsbury House
74–77 Great Russell Street
London WC1B 3DA

Typeset by Faber and Faber
Printed and bound by CPI Group (UK) Ltd, Croydon, CR0 4YY

Series created by Working Partners Limited, London W6 0QT

A CIP record for this book
is available from the British Library

978–0–571–25985–4

2 4 6 8 10 9 7 5 3

Magic Toyshop

Ragbag Friends

By Jessie Little

Illustrated by Penny Dann

ff

faber and faber

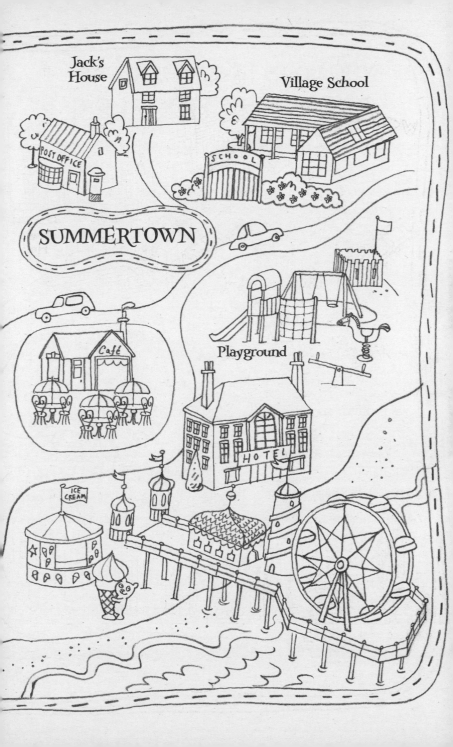

WHO LIVES IN SUMMERTOWN?
MEET THE HOOZLES!

This is
Willow and Toby

Here are Freddie
and Wobbly

Auntie Suzy
owns the toyshop!

The Hoozle Council - Grouchy, Wizard and Lovely

Frank the
Frankenhoozle
is new!

Nasty Croc is the
only mean Hoozle

Chapter One

Willow huddled close to Toby, her
Hoozle bear, and glanced at her
little brother. 'You're not frightened,
are you, Freddie?' she asked. They
were watching *Funky Frankenstein* in
the cosy sitting room above Auntie
Suzy's toy shop.

Freddie didn't take his eyes
off the TV. "Course not,' he said.
'Cartoons aren't real.' He was
lying on the floor, cuddling his lion
Hoozle, Wobbly. 'Dr Frankenstein

made a monster man out of bits
and pieces joined together.'

'Oh, look,' said Willow, 'the
monster man is sad because he
hasn't got a friend.' She kissed the
top of Toby's soft blue head. 'I'm
never lonely,' she whispered, 'because
I've got you.'

Toby checked that Freddie wasn't
looking, then slipped his paw into
Willow's hand. Almost nobody else
knew the astonishing Hoozle secret –
that they were alive! And there were
lots of them, too. Many children

in Summertown owned a Hoozle. They were all made in the toy shop by Auntie Suzy, on her pink sewing machine.

Feet thumped up the stairs and Willow's friend, Jack, appeared in the doorway with his purple tartan elephant Hoozle tucked under his arm. He waved its trunk at Willow. She waved Toby's paw and said, 'Hi, Bouncer. Hi, Jack.'

Willow made room for Bouncer on the sofa next to Toby, so they could whisper to each other while

she and Jack chatted. She loved
having a friend who knew the
Hoozle secret.

Jack sat beside her, and said,
'Are you looking forward to the
recycling fair tomorrow? The stalls
are set up in our field already.'

'I've thought about it all day,'

said Willow. 'We're even watching a cartoon about a recycled monster! I can't wait to come to your house for dinner, so I can see what's happening.'

'I've brought a poster for the toy shop, to tell people about the fair,' said Jack.

They ran downstairs. Auntie Suzy was busy, but when Jack waved his poster, she nodded and passed him some sticky-tack. As the poster went up, curious customers asked about the fair.

'It'll be brilliant,' said Jack. 'People can bring rubbish for recycling and take things they want to use, and you can swap clothes and shoes and books or *anything*.'

'People will be selling things made out of recycled materials,' said Willow. 'You should all come.'

As she spoke, Willow spotted a
movement on the shelf above the
counter. An owl-shaped Hoozle,
called Wizard, was flapping a
wingtip to attract her attention.
He never normally moved when
people were around, so this must
be important. She mouthed,

'What?' at Wizard.

He pointed to some people crowding round a low shelf, so Willow went over.

'It's weird!' said a woman. 'What's it supposed to be?'

Willow wiggled to the front. Jack squeezed in behind her. On the shelf sat a strange-looking toy. It was a sort of bear, with different-coloured button eyes. Its coat was made of different scraps of fabric. Nothing matched. When Willow picked it up, it rustled.

'It sounds like it's stuffed with paper,' said Jack. 'I think it's supposed to be a Hoozle, because there's a pocket on the front.'

Willow drew a sharp breath. 'That pocket couldn't have a pocket heart in it – the top has been stitched closed.'

A Hoozle owner always put something special in the Hoozle's pocket. It was a symbol of the love between them. A Hoozle without a pocket heart soon became dull and sad.

Willow felt sorry for the little
bear, especially when the boy said, 'I
wouldn't want a weird, ugly Hoozle
that looks like it's made of rubbish.'
He turned away.

'Wait! Hoozles are adorable,'

Willow told the people.

'They're soft and lovable and . . . and . . . look! This is Toby. He's not weird or made of rubbish.'

Jack showed them Bouncer. 'This is my Hoozle. He's my best toy.'

One or two customers stroked Toby and Bouncer before moving off. Jack looked closely at the weird Hoozle-like toy. 'There's something suspicious about this,' he said.

Willow nodded. 'And when suspicious things happen, we

know exactly who to
watch out for.'

They looked at each
other, nodded, and said together,
'Croc!'

Chapter Two

'What's that mean orange Hoozle
up to now?' Willow said to Jack.
She tucked the strange Hoozle-type
bear under one arm and snuggled
Toby under the other. 'Let's take the
Hoozle Council upstairs and try to
work out what's going on.'

'I'll fetch them,' said Jack. He
went to the shelf above the counter
and picked up Wizard and the two
Hoozles who lived there with him.

As Willow led them upstairs, she
heard Bouncer telling the Hoozle
Council about the strange new
bear.

Toby and Bouncer settled on the round red rug on Willow's bedroom floor. Wizard and Grouchy, a cute penguin Hoozle, joined them. The third Council member, Lovely the pony, needed to stretch her legs first.

Her purple mane flew as she galloped wildly round the room.

Willow put the Hoozle-thing down, and examined it with a magnifying glass.

Toby climbed on her lap, so he

could look, too. 'It's all bits and pieces,' he rumbled.

Willow nodded. 'Just like Frankenstein's monster.'

'Ooh!' said Toby. 'It's a Frankenhoozle.'

Lovely stroked the Frankenhoozle with a purple hoof. 'Poor thing,' she said. 'A Frankenhoozle with no pocket heart. It's sad that he has no one special to love him.'

Willow noticed that Grouchy looked upset. 'Never mind,' she said, stroking his velvety wing.

'I'll unpick the stitches
that keep his pocket shut.
Then at least he'll look more
like a proper Hoozle.' She found
some scissors and began snipping.

'Don't prick it,' Grouchy said
anxiously.

'I won't,' said Willow. 'Just three
more stitches.' Snip. Snip. Snip. She
held up the odd little bear. 'There!'

The Frankenhoozle blinked one
eye.

Everybody said, '*Oh!*'

Willow was thrilled. She stood

the bear on the rug and said, 'Hello,
I'm Willow. This is Toby, and . . .'

The Frankenhoozle spun round
and round, looking at all the other
Hoozles. When he stopped, he
wobbled a little.

'Are you dizzy?' Willow asked gently.

'No,' said the Frankenhoozle. 'I'm not Dizzy. That's not my name. I haven't got a name.'

'Aaah, you need a name,' said Bouncer. 'What about Scrunchy?'

'Or Jolly?' said Wizard.

Grouchy suggested 'Bruno'. Toby thought of 'Growly', but none of the names really suited him.

Then Jack said, 'I know! Frank the Frankenhoozle! Hands up who likes that name.'

Hands, paws, wings, a hoof and a trunk shot up. 'I like Frank,' everybody said.

Frank put his paw up. 'I like me, too.'

Willow giggled. He was so lovable. She started to ask where he came from, but all the Hoozles wanted to talk to Frank.

'How long have you been made?' asked Bouncer.

Lovely nuzzled his ears. 'You're so colourful,' she said.

'Why are your eyes different

colours?' Grouchy asked.

'Hooooooot!' Wizard cried. 'Let Willow speak.'

Everyone was quiet.

'Thanks, Wizard,' said Willow.

'Frank, who made you?'

'I don't know his name,' said
Frank. 'But I know what he looks
like.' He moved stiffly across the
room to where Willow had dropped
her bright orange pyjamas. 'He's
this colour,' he said, 'and he's going
to make more.'

'*More*?' said Willow.

'Lots more,' said Frank, adding
proudly. 'Just like me!'

Willow put the Hoozle Council
back on their shelf and whispered,
'Bye. We're off to Jack's now.'

'Don't worry, we'll put a stop to Croc's mischief,' Jack added quietly.

'First, we need to find out *how* he's doing it,' said Willow, 'before we can stop him.'

They said goodbye to Auntie Suzy, and walked along the sea front towards Jack's house. Frank was snuggled beside Toby in

Willow's backpack. She
could hear him asking funny
questions, like, 'Is this our bed?'

Toby kept giggling, but Willow
was busy thinking. 'Croc can't have
used Auntie Suzy's sewing machine,'
she said. 'She's the only person who
can work it.'

Jack shrugged. 'He could have
used any machine, anywhere.' He
pointed to a nearby shop. 'Look.
"Tracy Naylor, the Summertown
Tailor". She'll have a sewing
machine, for sure.'

Willow grinned. 'Tracy's a friend of Auntie Suzy.' They went inside.

'Willow, what luck!' said Tracy, when she saw Willow walk through the door. 'I need someone to try out my latest dress design. You'll be perfect.' She dashed to the back of the shop.

'Look,' Toby growled in Willow's ear. 'There's her sewing machine.'

Tracy pulled a bundle of polka-dotted material from the work table and hurried back

to Willow. 'There. What do you
think?'

Willow stroked the silky pink and
orange dress. 'It's gorgeous.'

'Oh, hello Toby,' said Tracy, reaching over Willow's shoulder and giving his paw a little shake.

Willow introduced Jack, Bouncer and Frank.

Tracy put her head on one side. 'Frank's a bit . . . different, isn't he?' She looked closer. 'He's very sweet, though.'

'We think so, too,' said Willow. 'I'll try the dress on now, if you like.'

Before she went into the changing room, Willow gave Jack her backpack. 'Look round the sewing machine for clues,' she said. 'Toby's got sharp eyes. He'll help you.'

She put the dress on, then walked up and down, like a model.

Tracy looked at it carefully. 'I need to make some changes,' she said, kneeling down. 'Hold still, while I pin the side seams.'

Willow looked over Tracy's head. Toby was examining the sewing machine, while Bouncer and Jack looked beneath the work table. Frank climbed up to look in the rubbish bin and almost fell in

head first. Luckily, Bouncer grabbed
his legs and pulled him back.

Willow smothered a giggle.

Tracy stood up. 'All done. You can
take it off now.'

Willow slipped into the changing room to put her own dress back on. When she came out, she was greeted by Jack, with four Hoozles in his arms and a big grin on his face.

Toby held a large piece of fluff between his paws. Orange fluff! So Croc had been here, making Frankenhoozles.

All we have to do, Willow thought, *is come back here and catch him. We must stop him using that machine.*

'You're a great model, Willow,'

said Tracy. 'I think this design is going to be a big success. And, as a thank you, this dress is for you once I've fixed the seams.'

'Wow, thanks!' said Willow.

Tracy sat down at her work table. After a moment, she shook her head. 'That's odd. My machine's not working,' she said. 'I'll have to pop the dress into Suzy's shop once it's repaired.'

They said goodbye and, just before Willow closed the door, she saw Tracy shake her head again and say, 'Most mysterious. It was working just fine yesterday.'

'Not mysterious at all,' Willow said crossly to Jack. 'Croc broke that machine. He can't use it again, so he'll go somewhere else. We'll have to find out where before we can stop him.'

Chapter Three

Toby patted Willow's neck. 'Maybe other shops have sewing machines?'

Frank pointed to a window. 'Is that a sewing thing?'

Willow giggled. 'No, it's a vacuum cleaner.'

'Oh,' said Frank. 'Well, what about that?'

'No, you funny little thing,' said Willow. 'That's a TV. But look there!'

Outside Adam's Furniture Store, a signboard said, 'Curtains made to measure.'

'They'll have a machine,' she cried. 'Come on.' She led them in.

Mr Adam smiled. 'Hello, Willow!' he said. 'How's Aunt Suzy?'

'Fine, thanks,' said Willow. She could hardly concentrate, because she'd just spotted an orange tail

poking out from beneath a leather
armchair. Croc must have seen the
sign as well! She nudged Jack.

He nodded. He'd seen it too. 'Er,
we're having a recycling
fair in the field next to
our house, Mr Adam,'

he said. 'We wondered if you have anything to recycle? Something in your store room, maybe?'

'There's some lampshades that could do with re-covering,' said Mr Adam. 'Let's go upstairs and find them.'

Jack gave his backpack to Willow and followed Mr Adam.

Willow shot across to the leather armchair but Croc was gone.

She let Toby and Bouncer out of the backpacks to help her search. Willow spotted movement at the

back of the shop and
they all rushed across.
Frank ran after them,
but one leg was longer
than the other, so he
ended up going round
in circles.

At the very back of the shop, a long row of brightly coloured curtain samples hung from ceiling to floor. Willow was just thinking what a perfect hiding place that was, when one curtain moved. Something was behind it! Willow signalled to Toby and Bouncer and pointed to the bulge. They stood ready to catch the crocodile.

She pulled the curtain aside.

'Ah ha!' she cried. But it wasn't a wriggly orange crocodile. It was their cute, rustly Frankenhoozle.

'I'm not Croc,' said Frank. 'He's in the big brown thing. Come and see.' He tottered off between rows of sofas, with Toby, Bouncer and Willow following. 'There,' he said, pointing to a grandfather clock.

'How can Croc be inside the clock, Frank?' Willow asked.

Frank blinked. 'He's in its tummy.'

Willow put her hand on the little door to the clock. 'Ready? One . . . two . . . three . . .'

'GO!' cried Croc's voice. The door flew open and he leapt out,

over Willow's shoulder, and boomp!
Right on top of Frank.

Frank wrestled with him just long
enough for Willow to recover and
pull him off the Frankenhoozle.

'Got you!' she declared, holding
the wriggling crocodile up in the air.

Chapter Four

'Let me go!' cried Croc. 'Put me down!'

'What are you up to?' Willow demanded.

Croc laughed. 'I'm making ugly Hoozles out of old rubbish,' he said. 'Soon there'll be more of my Hoozles than your Auntie Suzy's ones.'

'But I'll make sure you can't use Mr Adam's machine,' said Willow, 'so you can't make any more.'

'Ha! That won't stop me,' crowed Croc. 'I know another machine. I'll make lots more and all their pockets will be sewn up tight, so no one can put a pocket heart in there.

Children won't want Hoozles any more. They'll NEVER be loved! '

Willow heard Toby gasp. He and Bouncer looked angry. 'That Croc!' said Toby. 'He'll upset Frank, saying things like that.'

But Frank wasn't upset. He stuck his chin out. 'I'm *not* ugly; I'm a funny little thing,' he said. 'That's what Willow called me. And I want a pocket heart, so I can be like other Hoozles.'

As Willow reached down to pick Frank up, Croc saw his chance.

He lashed his tail and broke free of
her grip.

'Naah na-na
naah na!' he
shouted as he
tore outside.

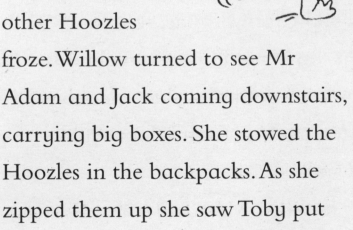

Suddenly, the
other Hoozles
froze. Willow turned to see Mr
Adam and Jack coming downstairs,
carrying big boxes. She stowed the
Hoozles in the backpacks. As she
zipped them up she saw Toby put
his arm round Frank.

'We found twelve lampshades, Willow,' said Mr Adam. 'I'll drop them round to the fair tomorrow, to save you carrying them.'

As he stacked the boxes, Willow quickly told Jack what had happened.

'So Croc's outside,' said Jack. 'Well, he won't get in here tonight. Mr Adam's got brand-new electronic steel shutters for his door and windows.'

Just then, Mr Adam called, 'Closing time, you two.'

'We'd better go,'
said Jack. 'Mum
will be wondering
where we are. See
you tomorrow, Mr
Adam.' As they
walked out the door,
Mr Adam locked up after them. 'At
least Croc won't be able to make
Frankenhoozles in there,' Jack said.

'But he said he knows another
machine,' said Willow. 'Oh, Jack,
where can it be?'

49

While Jack's mum cooked dinner,
Willow helped sort out piles of
recycling materials.

'This is the last lot,' said Jack.
'There's stacks more upstairs, already
sorted.'

There were different boxes for

fabrics, zips, plastics, paper, shoes,
and there was even a box for boxes!
Willow looked through a big basket
of things people had made to sell.
She surprised Jack's tabby cat, Fizz,
who'd curled up on some jumpers
for a snooze.

When dinner was ready, they left Toby, Bouncer and Frank to chat on Jack's bed, and ran downstairs, along a blue-painted corridor, down more stairs, and across the hall to the kitchen.

As she ate, Willow thought hard about where there could possibly be a sewing machine that Croc could use in secret. Jack was quiet, so she guessed he was thinking, too. She hadn't realised how hungry she was. 'That was lovely,' she said.

'Recycling gives you an appetite.'

'So does Croc-hunting,' Jack whispered.

'What was that?' his mum asked, sending Willow and Jack into fits of giggles.

After cherry pie and ice cream, they went back upstairs. Toby and Bouncer were playing marbles with Fizz the cat. Frank was fast asleep. 'He's having a Hoozle snoozle,' said Toby, covering him with a corner of the duvet.

After a while, Jack's mum called
them for hot chocolate. 'Drink
that before we take Willow home,'
she said. 'It'll help you get a good
night's sleep, so you'll have lots of
energy for the fair tomorrow.

I'll carry on sorting until you're ready, Willow. No hurry.'

When they'd finished their hot chocolate, Willow said, 'I'll fetch Toby and Frank. Won't be a moment.' She headed down the corridor.

Turn right . . . she thought, *or maybe left . . . oh dear. Which way was Jack's room?*

A flight of steps took Willow into a blue corridor. But it wasn't the one she'd been in before. She found more stairs that *looked* familiar, but

the landing at the top
was dark. As she turned back,
she heard a noise – a whirring
sound. In fact, it was rather like
the clatter of a sewing machine.
Willow pressed her ear to a door. It
was in there!

Slowly, she turned the handle.
The noise stopped, and there was
a *thump*! as if something had fallen
to the floor. As she peered into
the small dark room, she felt Fizz
scurry past her. On a table by the
window, in the moonlight, stood

a sewing machine. Beside it was a
heap of objects.

Willow switched on the light and
gasped.

Lined up by the sewing machine
were ten . . . fifteen . . . no, *twenty*
Frankenhoozles.

Chapter Five

Willow felt the sewing machine.
It was warm. She remembered the
scurrying creature. *That wasn't Fizz,*
she thought. *It was Croc!*

She examined the
Frankenhoozles. Some had four
eyes, some had one. Two had no

nose at all, and a yellow giraffe had ears like a rabbit.

The room was full of boxes of recycling stuff, stacked ready for the fair. Willow lifted a lid to find squares of different fabrics, cut out ready for someone to make patchwork. Another box was full of threads and balls of wool. A third held buttons, ribbons and zips. So that was what Croc had used to create the Frankenhoozles. She must tell Jack.

Willow ran along the corridor.

Wrong way. She ran back past
the sewing room to some stairs,
but they went up, not down.

In the end, she gave up and
yelled, 'Ja-ack!

I'm lost!'

As soon as he found her, she told him, 'Croc is somewhere in the house. Come and see.'

When Jack saw the Frankenhoozles, he smacked his forehead. 'I completely forgot Mum's sewing machine.' He peered at the Frankenhoozles. 'They're quite cute, aren't they? In a wonky sort of way.'

'Come *on*,' said Willow. 'We have to find Croc.'

Just then, they heard a loud meow from outside in the garden.

They rushed to the window to see
Croc cornered by Fizz the cat.

They hurried
down the stairs and
into the kitchen
where Jack's mum
was waiting.
'Ready to go?'

'Almost,' said Willow.
'I'll just pop outside for a moment.
I've lost something.'

As they went into the garden, Jack
grinned. 'So you lost something, did
you?'

Willow laughed. 'It's the truth!' she said. 'I lost Croc.'

They searched beneath bushes, up trees, behind flower pots, but there was no sign of the naughty Hoozle.

'Ow!' said Jack, holding his face.

'What's the matter?' asked Willow. 'Have you been stung?'

He bent to pick something up. 'No, I wasn't stung. I was hit – by a *peanut*.'

Willow turned slowly. Sitting on the bird table, grinning cheekily, was Croc!

'Yaaah! Can't catch me!' he taunted. 'And you can't stop me making fake Hoozles. There are plenty more sewing machines. I'm too clever, I am!' He sprang on to the whirly washing line, and swung on to the fence. A second later he'd disappeared.

'He's gone,' Willow said miserably. 'Oh, Jack, there's nothing we can do to stop him. You heard what he said – there are plenty more sewing machines. He'll never give up.'

They trudged back to the house.

'Let's fetch Toby and Frank,' said Willow.

They went upstairs and told their Hoozles what had happened. No one knew what to do.

'I feel so sad for the

Frankenhoozles,' Toby growled. 'I
know they don't look quite right,
but you don't have to look perfect
to be nice.' He turned to Frank.
'Bouncer and I like you a lot.'

Frank smiled his crooked smile
and patted his pocket. 'It's a good
feeling when someone likes you,
isn't it?'

'Can I look?'
Willow asked. She
peeped into
Frank's pocket.
There was a

green marble in there! She looked at Toby. 'Did you do that?'

He nodded shyly. 'I know I'm not his owner, but I thought it would be kind.'

Willow smiled. 'It was very kind. And you're the best little bear there ever was.' Then she said, 'OH!'

'What?' said Jack.

'That's it!' Willow said. 'We've got to show Croc that his plan won't work. We have to show him that all toys can be loved, even if they're not perfect. Hmm,' she went on. 'I have a plan, but it's a little risky.' She looked at Jack. 'What we need is the Frankenhoozles – and scissors.'

Chapter Six

Auntie Suzy tucked Willow and
Toby into bed, and kissed each
forehead. 'Goodnight.'

'Night,' said Willow. As soon as
the door closed, she pulled a big bag
out from under the bed. She and
Toby unpacked ten Frankenhoozles,

then Willow got to work with the scissors, snipping open each little pocket. One by one, the Frankenhoozles came to life!

Toby looked after them while she snipped. 'Aah,' he kept saying, or, 'This one's so cute.' When a duck-shaped Frankenhoozle tripped over its own big feet, it tumbled off the bed and did a roly-poly right across the floor. Toby giggled. 'That one thinks it's an acrobat!'

When all the Hoozles were done, Willow made them a big blankety bed on the rug, then snuggled in her own bed with Frank and Toby. 'Night-night,' she said and kissed them both. 'Night-night, Frankenhoozles.'

Frank fell asleep immediately, but Toby said softly, 'Willow?'

She looked down into his dear little face. 'You're sad. What's wrong?'

'The Frankenhoozles haven't got anyone to kiss them goodnight,' he said.

Willow climbed out of bed to

drop ten goodnight kisses on ten
funny little faces, then they all went
to sleep.

After breakfast, Willow put Toby
and Frank in her backpack and
grabbed her bag of Frankenhoozles.
'Bye,' she said. 'I'm
off to the recycling
fair.'

  'I'll bring Freddie
later,' said Auntie
Suzy. She glanced
at the wriggly

Frankenhoozle bag, but didn't say anything. Willow thought she had probably guessed it was something to do with a Hoozle adventure!

At the recycling fair, Willow put the Frankenhoozle bag under a table, and helped Jack set out the handmade things. There were hats and scarves knitted with wool from old jumpers. There were plaited mats made from plastic carrier bags, and even a model ship made from old nails.

Jack yawned. 'I had a rotten

night,' he said. 'When I unpicked the
Frankenhoozles' pockets, they all
came to life.'

'Good,' said Willow.

'But Bouncer and I couldn't
sleep with ten daft Frankenhoozles
tottering round the room,' said Jack.
'They kept bumping into things,
and all we heard was "Oof!" and
"Oops!" and bumps and giggles.
I finally tucked them up with a
blanket in my model castle, but this
morning I found two of them fast
asleep in my slippers.'

Willow
laughed.
'Well, they're
here now.
We'll soon
see if our plan
works.' She chose a table. 'Let's set
the Frankenhoozles out here.' They
arranged them, and Willow told
them to keep still. 'I'm worried
they'll forget and wander off,' she
whispered to Toby.

'They can't help being a bit silly,'
he replied. 'Don't get cross with them.'

Willow couldn't imagine getting cross. Just looking at those appealing, lop-sided little faces made her smile.

When Auntie Suzy appeared and saw the Frankenhoozles, she raised her eyebrows in surprise and said, 'Goodness! Someone's been busy. And aren't they sweet!' Then she and Willow shared a special smile.

But Willow was anxious. What if

people thought they were *too*
peculiar? Suppose no one
bought them?

She soon had her answer. A
small girl dragged her mum to
the Frankenhoozle table. 'Can I
have one? squealed the girl. 'Can I,
please?'

Her mum asked Willow how
much they cost, then nodded. 'Yes,
Rosie, you can have one!'

Rosie chose a cat with a huge
pink nose and a stumpy tail. 'He's
so sweet,' she said. 'I'll call him Bitsy,
cos he's made of bits and pieces.'

Willow took the money and gave
Rosie a penny change. When she
explained about putting something

special in Bitsy's pocket, Rosie
said, 'I'll put this penny in, then I'll
always remember the first time I
saw him.'

Another girl ran over. 'Hi,
Rosie,' she said. 'Oh, that's so cute.
Mummeeeee, look! Frankenhoozles!'

Suddenly, Willow and Jack
were selling Frankenhoozle after
Frankenhoozle. Children wandered
round showing off their new
toys, and soon there was just one
Frankenhoozle left – a nanny goat
with a cute, lop-sided smile.

'If Croc sees children all
around Summertown loving their
Frankenhoozles,' Willow said
thoughtfully, 'do you think that will
be enough to stop him bothering to
make any more?'

Just then a man asked Jack for the

goat with the lop-sided smile. 'My son's hurt his knee,' he said. 'This will cheer him up.'

'I hope so,' said Willow. She and Jack watched as the man gave the boy the Frankenhoozle. 'Oh look! He's stopped crying already.'

The table was empty and the fair was almost over. Willow put her backpack on. Then she had an awful thought. 'Where's Frank? Jack, we must have sold Frank! Oh, I didn't say goodbye,' she wailed.

Toby poked her ear and whispered, 'Look down there.'

Frank was sitting on the grass, hugging the table leg, with his eyes squeezed shut. 'Don't swap me for money,' he cried.

Willow unpeeled his paws and cuddled him. 'Don't you want a nice home, too?' she whispered. She knew he was upset because his voice was hiccupy.

'I want to stay with my friends in the toy shop,' he said.

Toby reached across Willow's
shoulder and stroked Frank's cheek.
'We want you to stay, too.'

Frank sniffed happily. 'Do you
really?'

'Of course we do,' said Willow. 'We
all love Frank, don't we?'

'Yay!' cried Toby, Bouncer and
Jack, and even
Frank joined in.
Then Willow
tucked him in
her backpack
and Toby gave

him the biggest hug ever.

Willow noticed Jack staring at some empty boxes. 'What is it?' she asked.

'Croc's over there between those boxes,' he said. 'Watching.'

Willow glanced across. The orange Hoozle was looking absolutely furious.

Willow crouched down so no one could see, then she, Toby and Frank waved to him. 'Your Frankenhoozles are just as happy as any other Hoozle,' she called. 'And just as loved.'

Croc snapped his jaw, lashed his tail and stormed away.

Willow grinned. 'Come on. Let's get you Hoozles back home where you belong.'

Frank leaned his funny little face against her shoulder. 'I like belonging, Willow. Belonging makes me happy.'

Get ready for even more

Magic Toyshop adventures!